PEARL HARBOR

Robin Johnson

CRABTREE
Publishing Company
www.crabtreebooks.com

Crabtree Publishing Company
www.crabtreebooks.com

Author: Robin Johnson
Publishing plan research and development: Reagan Miller
Editors: Sonya Newland, Kathy Middleton
Proofreader: Wendy Scavuzzo
Photo Researcher: Robin Johnson/Sonya Newland
Original design: Tim Mayer (Mayer Media)
Book design: Clare Nicholas
Cover design: Ken Wright
Production coordinator and prepress technician: Ken Wright
Print coordinator: Katherine Berti

Produced for Crabtree Publishing Company by White-Thomson Publishing

Cover:
Shutterstock: Keith Tarrier

Photographs:
Alamy: War Posters: p. 41; Corbis: p. 40; **Getty Images:** pp. 15, 24–25; Gamma-Keystone via Getty Images: p. 7; Time & Life Pictures: p. 10; Moviepix: pp. 12–13; **Library of Congress:** pp. 14, 18, 28, 28–29, 31; **National Archives and Record Administration:** pp. 19, 34; **Shutterstock:** pinggr: pp. 1, 44–45; Charlesimage: p. 8; Bruce C. Murray: p. 23; Keith Tarrier: pp. 32–33; Dr. Alan Lipkin: p. 35; NeonLight: pp. 42–43; a katz: p. 44; **Superstock:** pp. 4–5; Universal Images Group: p. 6; The Art Archive: p. 9; ClassicStock.com: pp. 20–21; Buyenlarge: pp. 38–39; **Thinkstock:** tropicalpix: p. 37; **Topfoto:** The Granger Collection: pp. 16–17, 26–27; **Wikimedia:** NARA: pp. 1, 22–23; PhoM2c. Paul Queenan, USCG: p. 36.

Library and Archives Canada Cataloguing in Publication

Johnson, Robin (Robin R.), author
Pearl Harbor / Robin Johnson.

(Crabtree chrome)
Includes index.
Issued in print and electronic formats.
ISBN 978-0-7787-1367-8 (bound).--ISBN 978-0-7787-1403-3 (pbk.).--
ISBN 978-1-4271-8981-3 (pdf).--ISBN 978-1-4271-8975-2 (html)

1. Pearl Harbor (Hawaii), Attack on, 1941--Juvenile literature.
I. Title. II. Series: Crabtree chrome

D767.92.J64 2014 j940.54'26693 C2014-903917-4
C2014-903918-2

Library of Congress Cataloging-in-Publication Data

Johnson, Robin (Robin R.)
Pearl Harbor / Robin Johnson.
pages cm. -- (Crabtree chrome)
Includes index.
ISBN 978-0-7787-1367-8 (reinforced library binding) --
ISBN 978-0-7787-1403-3 (pbk.) --
ISBN 978-1-4271-8981-3 (electronic pdf) --
ISBN 978-1-4271-8975-2 (electronic html)
1. Pearl Harbor (Hawaii), Attack on, 1941--Juvenile literature. 2. World War, 1939-1945--Causes--Juvenile literature. 3. Japan--Foreign relations--United States--Juvenile literature. 4. United States--Foreign relations--Japan--Juvenile literature. I. Title.

D767.92.J63 2014
940.54'26693--dc23

2014028063

Crabtree Publishing Company
www.crabtreebooks.com 1-800-387-7650

Printed in Canada/122022/CPC20221201

Published in Canada
Crabtree Publishing
616 Welland Ave.
St. Catharines, ON
L2M 5V6

Published in the United States
Crabtree Publishing
347 Fifth Ave
Suite 1402-145
New York, NY 10016

Published in the United Kingdom
Crabtree Publishing
Maritime House
Basin Road North, Hove
BN41 1WR

Published in Australia
Crabtree Publishing
Unit 3-5
Currumbin Court
Capalaba QLD 4157

Contents

The Road to War

Enemy Aircraft

On December 7, 1941, sailors in the U.S. Navy at Pearl Harbor woke to a terrible shock. The sky was swarming with aircraft marked with the Rising Sun. Bombs were raining down and exploding all around them. The United States was under attack by Japan!

▲ *The attack on Pearl Harbor came as a complete surprise. Men scrambled to escape as the battleships went up in smoke.*

Surprise Attack

Japan destroyed a dozen U.S. warships and killed more than 2,400 men that day. Although World War II had been raging in Europe for two years, the surprise strike shocked Americans—and the rest of the world. Striking back, the United States declared war on Japan the next day and joined the fighting in World War II.

Pearl Harbor was a U.S. naval base on the island of Oahu, Hawaii. A naval base is a port where warships are stored, repaired, and stocked with supplies. At the time of the attack, nearly a hundred ships were docked in Pearl Harbor—almost the entire U.S. **fleet** in the Pacific Ocean.

fleet: a group of warships that sail and work together

Trouble Brewing

Tension had been building between Japan and the United States for many years. The trouble started during the Great Depression. The Great Depression was a period when the worldwide **economy** was very poor. It began in 1929 and lasted for ten years. During that time, a lot of businesses failed and many people did not have jobs.

▶ *During the Great Depression, people waited in long lines for free food. They could not afford to buy the fine items that were shipped from Japan.*

Hit Hard

Japan was hit hard by the Great Depression. It was an island nation with only a few natural resources. Its economy relied on trading goods with other countries. However, the United States wanted Americans to buy products made in America to boost its own economy. In 1930, the U.S. government raised the taxes it charged other countries to ship goods into the United States. That way, fewer products from other countries could compete with American-made products. Other countries soon raised their fees, too.

▼ *Worldwide trading slowed down during the Great Depression, leaving Japan in serious trouble.*

Japan needed resources to fuel its factories and make goods. It imported oil, coal, iron, steel, and rubber from other countries. Japan exported silk and other fine goods to places around the world.

economy: the money and resources in a country

The Empire Strikes Back

Japan had many factories, but it needed oil and other resources to run them. When trading costs rose, Japan could not afford to buy the resources it needed. So Japan's emperor, Hirohito, decided to grow Japan's **empire** instead. The Japanese began invading nearby countries to get their resources.

▶ *Hirohito became Emperor of Japan in 1926. He was determined to improve Japan's economy, even if it meant war.*

> **"One man's life or death is a matter of no importance. All that matters is the Empire."**
>
> Admiral Isoroku Yamamoto, the leader of Japan's Navy

Attacking for Oil

In 1931, Japan conquered a part of China called Manchuria. Six years later, the Japanese began storming the rest of China and taking it by force. In 1941, they invaded countries in Southeast Asia, including Cambodia, Laos, and Vietnam. Japan needed resources—and would do whatever it took to get them.

▲ *Japanese soldiers invaded China in 1937, starting a war that continued until the end of World War II in 1945.*

empire: a large area of land that is ruled by one leader

No More Oil

U.S. president Franklin D. Roosevelt did not agree with Japan's attacks on Southeast Asia. He stopped American trade with Japan in July 1941. At the time, Japan got most of its oil and other resources from the United States. With the **embargo** in place, Japan could not grow its economy, its army, or its empire.

▼ *These oil barrels are piled up outside the docks during the oil embargo on Japan.*

Patrolling the Pacific

The U.S. Navy sent ships to keep the peace in Southeast Asia. The Japanese believed that if U.S. ships no longer patrolled the Pacific Ocean between Japan and the United States, Japan could invade other countries and get the oil it needed. To stop the patrols, Japan decided to destroy the U.S. fleet at Pearl Harbor.

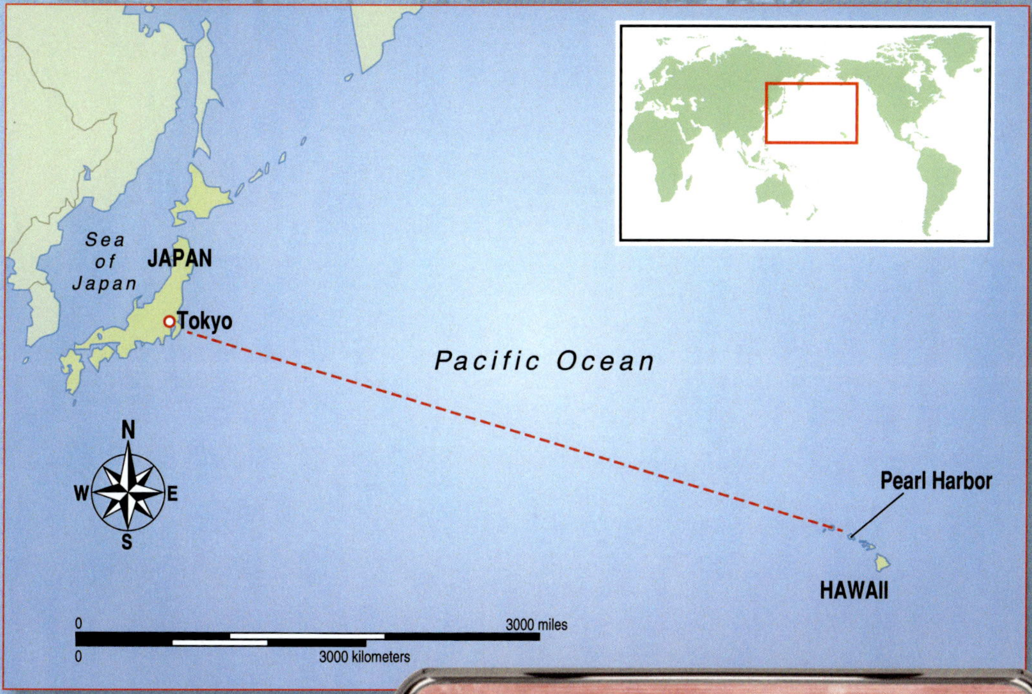

▲ *This map shows the position of Pearl Harbor in Hawaii in relation to Japan.*

World War II began in Europe on September 1, 1939, when Germany invaded Poland. Soon Britain, France, and many other countries were at war. In 1941, the world was watching the fighting in Europe. No one noticed Japan preparing to attack the United States.

embargo: a government order to stop trading with a country

Plan of Attack

Leading the Charge

Admiral Isoroku Yamamoto was in charge of Japan's navy. He began planning a daring **air raid** on Pearl Harbor in early 1941. His goal was to take the Pacific fleet out of action for at least six months. Yamamoto knew that the Japanese had to hit Pearl Harbor with a quick and crushing blow, or their risky plan would fail. Surprise was a key part of the attack. The United States must not see them coming.

▶ *Japanese airmen trained to hit precise targets in their fast, low-flying planes.*

Preparing for Battle

Admiral Yamamoto spent many months preparing his men for the air raid. He sent spies to Pearl Harbor to gather information about the target. He built models of the harbor and American warships and studied them with his men. Yamamoto ran drills in a shallow harbor in Japan that was similar to Pearl Harbor. At last, Japan was ready to strike.

Isoroku Yamamoto had studied and worked in the United States. He knew that Americans would not give up without a fight. Yamamoto also realized that Japan was no match for the United States. Japan had a strong, well-trained army, but America was bigger and had many more resources.

air raid: an attack by enemy planes

Advance Force

In mid-November, a fleet of Japanese submarines headed for Hawaii. Five of the subs carried small underwater craft called midget submarines. Midget subs held two men and two torpedoes. They were used to invade harbors and other small spaces. Japan would use the mini subs to sneak into Pearl Harbor and **ambush** the Americans by sea.

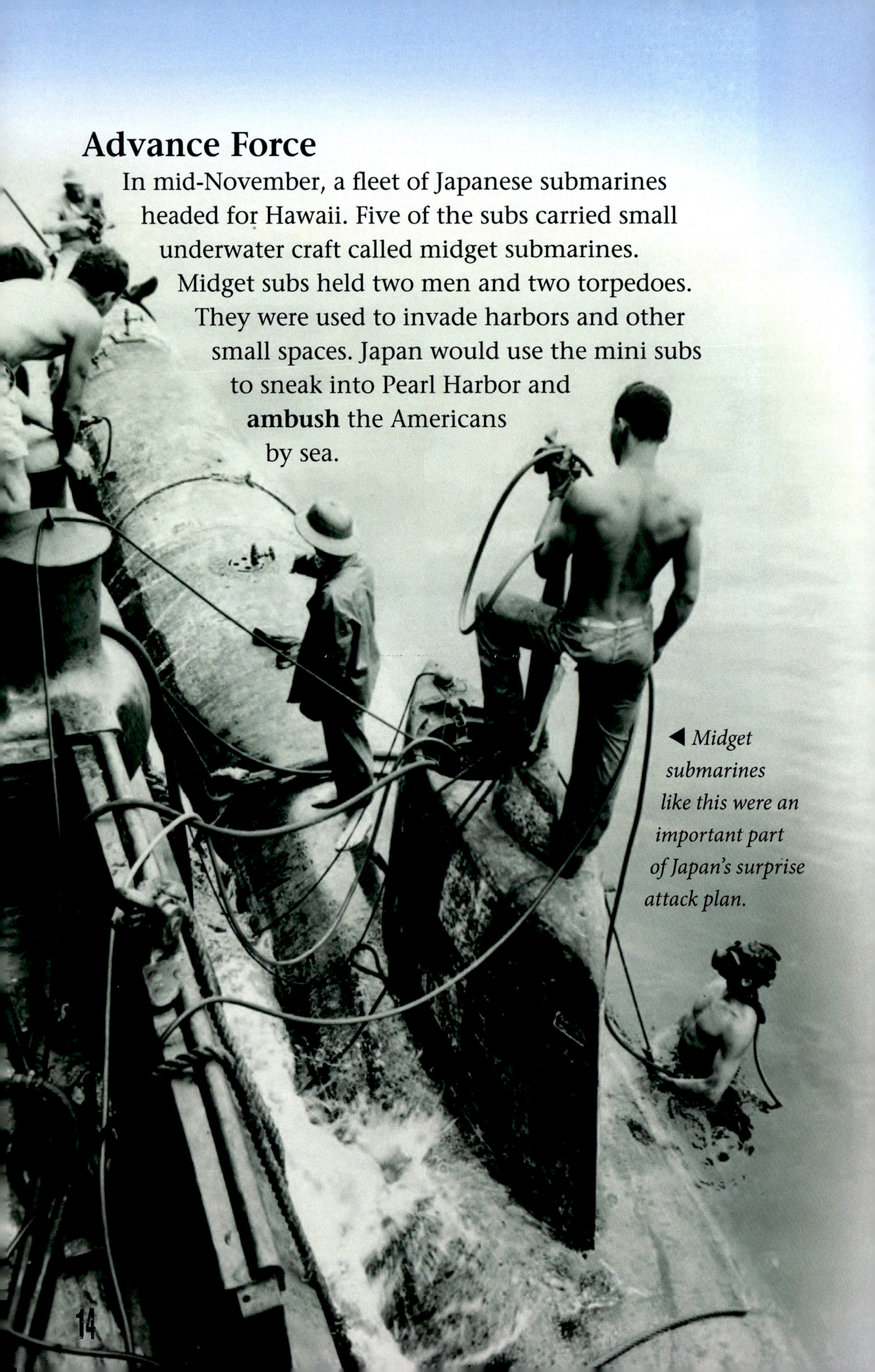

◀ *Midget submarines like this were an important part of Japan's surprise attack plan.*

Striking Force

On November 26, a fleet of more than 30 warships left Japan. Six massive ships, called aircraft carriers, transported hundreds of torpedo planes, bombers, and fighter planes. The planes took off from the ships and ambushed the Americans by air. The large Japanese fleet of ships dropped anchor about 274 miles (440 kilometers) from Pearl Harbor.

▲ *Japan sent battleships, cruisers, and destroyers to support and protect the aircraft carriers, and tankers to fuel the warships.*

About an hour before the air strike, an American destroyer called the USS *Ward* spied a midget submarine near Pearl Harbor. The Americans fired the first shots and sank the sub. The naval base at Pearl Harbor did not find out about the enemy submarine until the air raid was already underway.

ambush: to attack by surprise

Surprise Attack

The Calm Before the Storm

December 7, 1941, began like any normal Sunday at the Pearl Harbor naval base. The sailors ate breakfast in mess halls. Some prepared to raise the flag, while others got ready for church. Many men were still sleeping when their nightmare began at Pearl Harbor.

Japan is called "The Land of the Rising Sun." The name was given to the Japanese empire by Chinese rulers long ago, because Japan is east of China and closer to the sun when it rises.

Rising Sun

Around 7:55 a.m., Americans noticed planes flying in the distance. At first, they figured it was just a training drill. After all, the United States was not at war and had not been **alerted** to danger. As the planes got closer, they saw the Rising Sun on the sides of the planes. They knew then it was not a drill.

▼ *This picture shows Pearl Harbor just before the attack. The Japanese planned the assault for Sunday morning because they knew American sailors would be relaxing then.*

alerted: warned of danger

Air Raid!

Suddenly, the sky above Pearl Harbor was filled with Japanese aircraft! Dive bombers dipped low over the ships docked in the harbor. They began dropping bombs on the unsuspecting crews below. The sky flashed and shouts rang out as the first bombs smashed into the ships.

▲ *This photograph was taken by a Japanese pilot as he approached Pearl Harbor.*

> **"Even after I saw a huge fireball and cloud of black smoke rise ... and heard explosions, it did not occur to me that these were enemy planes. It was too incredible! Simply beyond imagination!"**
>
> Lee Soucy, a crewman on the USS *Utah*, a battleship sunk in Pearl Harbor

No Escape

The bombs woke the sleeping sailors in a hurry! They scrambled to get dressed and get to their posts. But the men were not prepared for battle. Their **ammunition** was locked up. Their ships were packed closely together in plain sight. The men were trapped in the harbor with no escape.

▼ *Admiral Husband Kimmel at Pearl Harbor sent an urgent message to the U.S. Navy fleet at 8:00 a.m.*

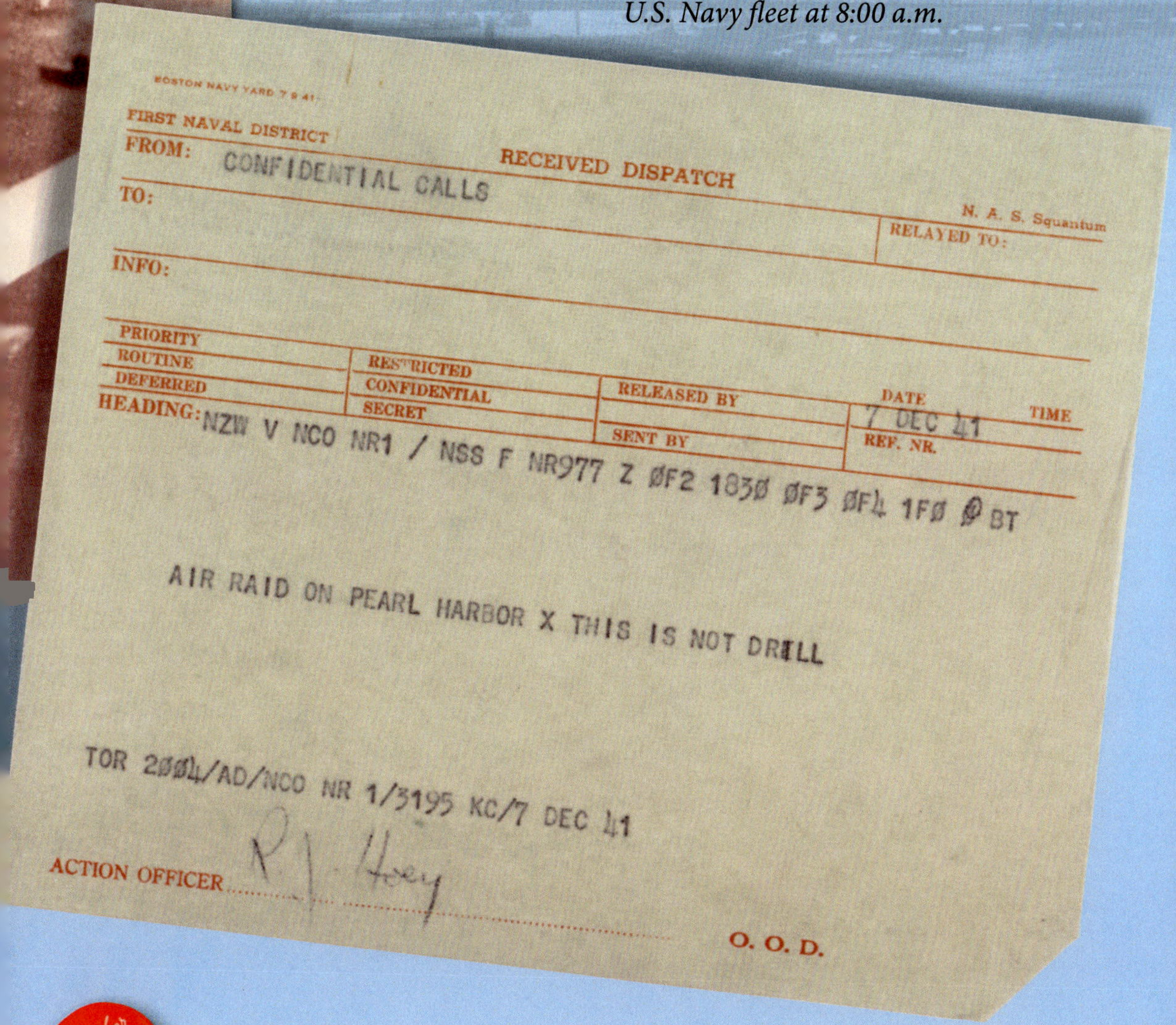

BOSTON NAVY YARD 7-9-41

FIRST NAVAL DISTRICT

RECEIVED DISPATCH

FROM: CONFIDENTIAL CALLS

N. A. S. Squantum

TO:

RELAYED TO:

INFO:

PRIORITY / ROUTINE / DEFERRED

RESTRICTED / CONFIDENTIAL / SECRET

RELEASED BY

SENT BY

DATE 7 DEC 41

TIME

REF. NR.

HEADING: NZW V NCO NR1 / NSS F NR977 Z ØF2 183Ø ØF3 ØF4 1FØ Ø BT

AIR RAID ON PEARL HARBOR X THIS IS NOT DRILL

TOR 2ØØ4/AD/NCO NR 1/3195 KC/7 DEC 41

ACTION OFFICER

O. O. D.

ammunition: bullets and shells fired from weapons

First Strike

Japanese planes targeted the American battleships first. Battleships were huge, powerful warships filled with people and weapons. Japan **bombarded** the battleships with underwater missiles dropped from torpedo planes. They also used fighter planes to destroy American aircraft before they could take off.

▼ *Many American fighter planes were parked in long rows at nearby airfields. American battleships were all lined up beside each other in Battleship Row. They were easy targets for Japan's skilled pilots.*

Fighting Back

Despite their shock, American sailors acted quickly. About five minutes into the attack, they began to fight back. Several American gunners reached their posts. They loaded anti-aircraft guns and tried to shoot down the Japanese planes. A handful of American fighter pilots reached their planes and took to the air. They shot down a few enemy aircraft but were greatly outnumbered by the Japanese.

"Smoke was spreading rapidly over the harbor. Very shortly the day became black as night; it was terrifying beyond means of description."

George Macartney Hunter, an officer on the USS *West Virginia*

bombarded: attacked repeatedly with bombs

Ball of Flames

At 8:10 a.m., a battleship called the USS *Arizona* was hit hard. A heavy bomb slammed through the ship's deck and into its **magazine**. More than a million pounds of explosives had been stored there. The ship burst into a giant ball of flames.

▼ *Thick black clouds filled the air as the USS* Arizona *went up in smoke.*

While planes bombarded battleships by air, a small fleet of midget submarines attacked the ships by sea. Most of the mini subs missed their targets and were sunk or taken by the United States, however. A Japanese sailor escaped from his damaged sub and was captured by the Americans. He became the first prisoner of war held by the United States in World War II.

Battleship Down

Less than ten minutes after it was hit, the mighty ship had sunk, with much of its crew still on board. Nearly 1,200 officers and crewmen were killed on the USS *Arizona* that day. It was the greatest loss of life on any warship in the history of the U.S. Navy.

▲ *The names of the men who went down with the USS* Arizona *are carved on a memorial at Pearl Harbor.*

magazine: a place where explosives are stored on a ship

Abandon Ship!

Another battleship called the USS *Oklahoma* was hit by torpedoes early in the attack. Some men **abandoned** the ship as it was starting to roll over. But they did not give up the fight. Braving gunfire from low-flying planes, the men climbed onto the nearby USS *Maryland* and continued to defend the harbor.

▼ *More than 400 men died when the USS* Oklahoma *capsized on Battleship Row.*

Down with the Ship

Just 12 minutes after it was hit, the USS *Oklahoma* capsized, or tipped over. Many men were trapped inside the huge battleship. Rescuers cut holes in the ship and tried to pull the men to safety. Some sailors were saved, but many were not. They went down with their ship in Pearl Harbor that day.

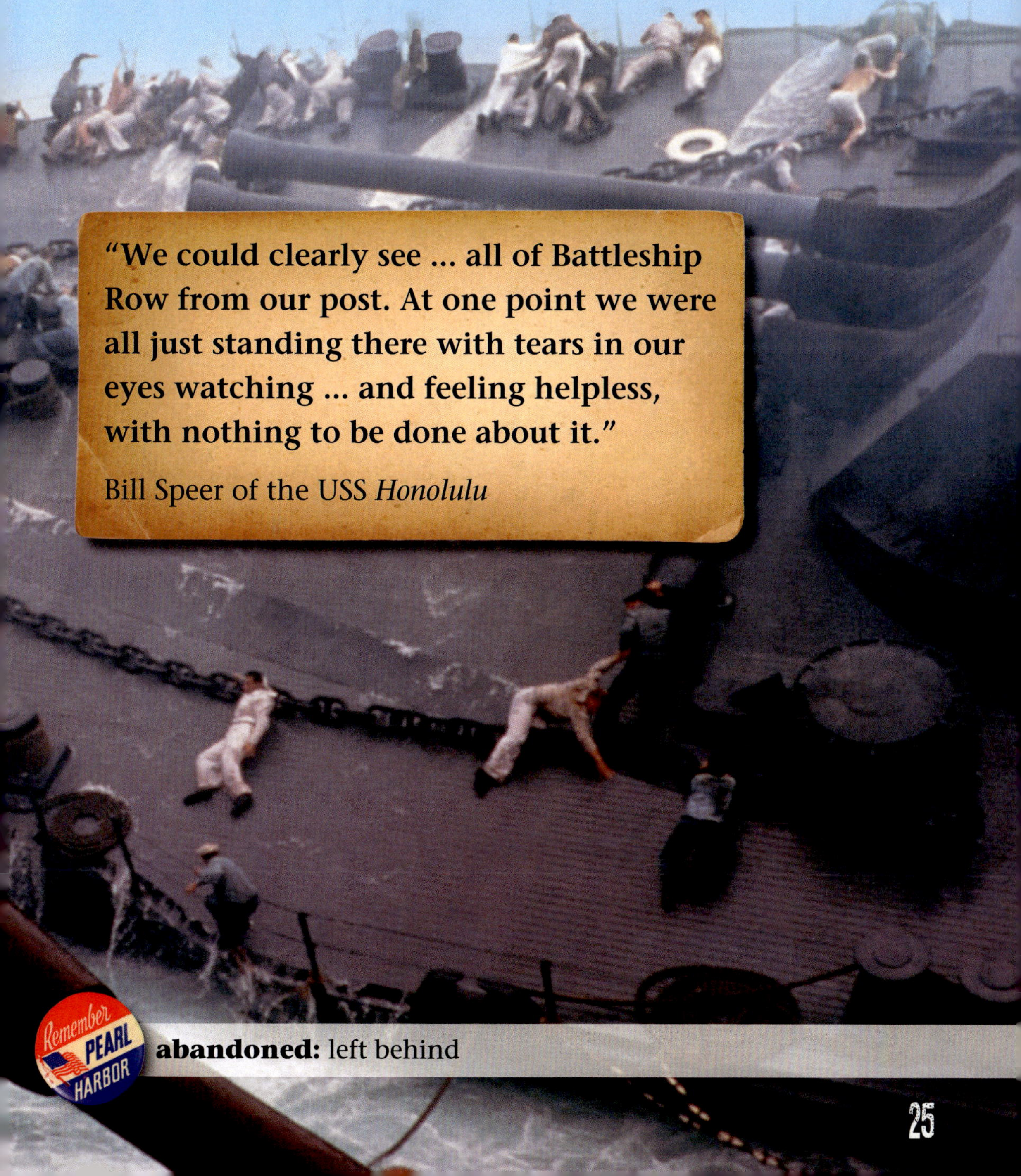

> **"We could clearly see ... all of Battleship Row from our post. At one point we were all just standing there with tears in our eyes watching ... and feeling helpless, with nothing to be done about it."**
>
> Bill Speer of the USS *Honolulu*

abandoned: left behind

Second Strike

There was a break in the bombing around 8:40 a.m. Then Japanese aircraft came back to finish what they had started. Some planes bombarded the battleships that were already in trouble. They pounded them with torpedoes again and again. Others targeted cruisers, destroyers, and other warships that had not been destroyed in the first wave of the attack.

▼ *The USS* Nevada *was the only battleship that tried to escape from the harbor that morning. Docked at the end of Battleship Row, it was not blocked in by other ships.*

Full Steam Ahead

Japanese dive bombers targeted a battleship that was trying to get away. The USS *Nevada* had raised anchor and was steaming out to sea. It was hit by a torpedo and several bombs along the way, however. The Americans were forced to **beach** their own ship so it would not sink and block the exit out of the harbor for other ships.

A total of 353 Japanese aircraft attacked Pearl Harbor that day, including 78 Mitsubishi A6M Zero planes. The Japanese Zero was a fast, lightweight fighter plane—and the terror of the Pacific. It could travel far from its carrier, make steep climbs and drops, dart around other aircraft, and hit targets from great distances.

beach: to run a ship onto shore

Picking up the Pieces

The Dead

By 9:45 a.m., Japanese bombers had left Pearl Harbor. The entire attack lasted less than two hours and left 2,403 Americans dead. Most were sailors who were on the ships when the bombs hit. Soldiers, airmen, marines, and **civilians** were also killed in the deadly air raid.

▲ *These civilians were killed when their car was hit with small pieces of exploding bombs during the attack. They were 8 miles (13 kilometers) away from Pearl Harbor.*

The Survivors

Some men survived the brutal attack but were seriously injured. Nearly 1,200 men were wounded in battle that day. Many were badly burned in the fiery blasts. Others had lost arms or legs when the bombs exploded. None of the survivors would ever be the same.

> **"It was just terrible. It was one of those things when you think, what's the world coming to?"**
>
> Horace Warden, Medical Officer on the USS *Breese*

▼ *These sailors are decorating the graves of men who died during the attack on Pearl Harbor.*

civilians: people who are not in the armed forces

The Damage

The U.S. Navy fleet was crushed at Pearl Harbor. A dozen ships were sunk or beached, including five huge battleships. Three battleships, three cruisers, three destroyers, and a number of other ships were damaged in the air raid. Nearly 200 American planes were also destroyed.

▲ *This map shows where the U.S. fleet was in Pearl Harbor that day, and how much damage was done. Battleships were large, armed warships, cruisers were smaller battleships, and destroyers were fast ships used to protect the fleet.*

Missing in Action

Luckily for the United States, there were no American aircraft carriers in the harbor that day. All three ships were out at sea. Important buildings—such as the power station and oil storage tanks—were also not hit in the attack. The United States would need its ships and supplies to strike back at Japan.

The attack on Pearl Harbor was a major victory for the Japanese. They lost just 64 men, 29 planes, and five midget submarines. The Japanese may have won the battle that day—but their attack brought a strong new enemy into the war.

▼ *Rescuers approach the burning USS* West Virginia, *trying to save the men trapped on board.*

victory: the act of winning

Other Targets

Pearl Harbor was not Japan's only target on December 7, 1941. Japanese forces also attacked several other islands in the western Pacific Ocean. They hit the U.S. territories of Guam, the Philippines, Wake Island, and Midway Island. They also attacked the British **colonies** of Hong Kong and Malaya.

In 1941, Hawaii was a territory of the United States. A territory is a part of a country that does not have full rights as a state. Hawaii became the 50th state of the United States on August 21, 1959.

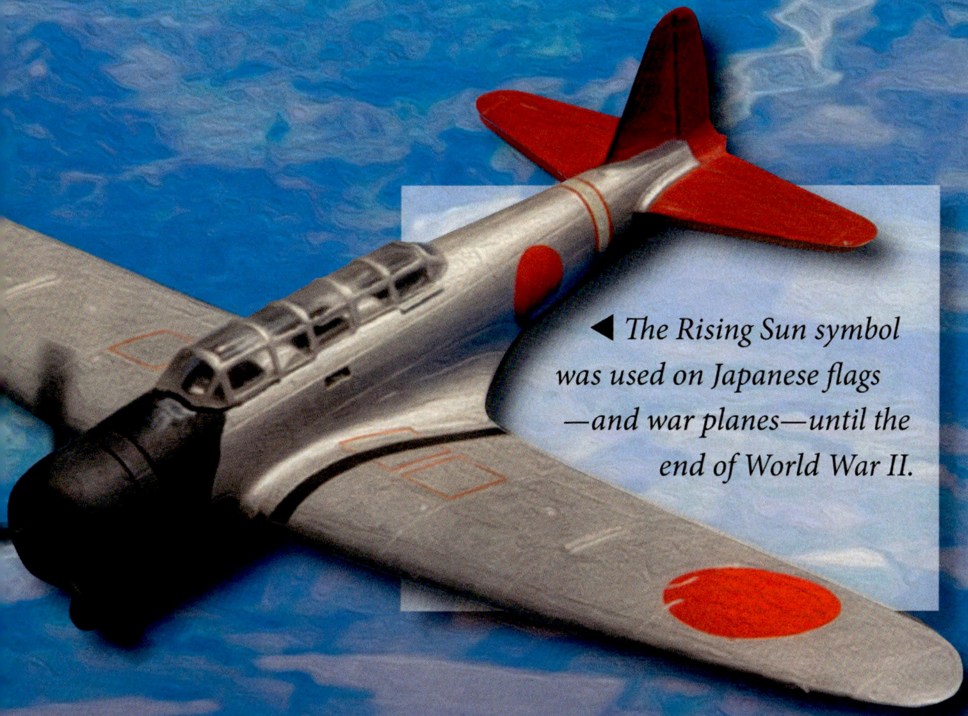

◀ *The Rising Sun symbol was used on Japanese flags—and war planes—until the end of World War II.*

Fight Plans

Japan planned to take over the islands and get control of their resources before the United States and Britain could strike back. Japanese planes dropped bombs on the islands. Then ground troops landed and captured the islands—all except one. Midway Island held off the Japanese troops and won the first American victory of World War II.

colonies: places ruled by faraway leaders

This Means War!

Down But Not Out

Japan had hoped that the attack on Pearl Harbor would break the Americans. Instead, it brought them roaring into World War II. Before the attack, the United States was fiercely divided. Some people were eager to fight in Europe, while others did not want to join a faraway war they felt did not concern them. The attack on Pearl Harbor brought Americans together with a shared goal—to get revenge on Japan.

▶ *Posters called for Americans to do their duty and avenge those who died at Pearl Harbor.*

"I fear that all we have done is awaken a sleeping giant."

Japanese Admiral Isoroku Yamamoto, who had warned what might happen if Japan provoked the United States into declaring war

A Day of Infamy

On December 8, President Roosevelt gave an important speech to the U.S. Congress, the only part of the government with the power to declare war on another country. Roosevelt called the day Pearl Harbor was attacked "a date which will live in **infamy**." He also said that Americans were "in grave danger" and urged Congress to take action. Later that day, the United States declared war on the Empire of Japan. Britain also declared war on Japan that day for attacks against its colonies.

▼ *Roosevelt planned his speech carefully, knowing that his words could change the course of history. Part of the speech is carved on a plaque in Washington, D.C.*

infamy: being famous for something bad

Call to Arms

On December 11, Germany and Italy declared war on the United States. The two countries were **allies** of Japan during World War II. These declarations of war drew Americans into the fight in Europe, too. The United States had no choice but to enter World War II and join forces with Great Britain and its allies to defeat Germany.

▼ *U.S. Marines land supplies on the Japanese island of Iwo Jima after it had been captured in a fierce battle.*

The Final Blow

American troops fought on land and at sea. The final blow to Japan came in August 1945. A new and extraordinarily powerful weapon called the atomic bomb was used for the first and only time in history. The United States dropped atomic bombs on the Japanese cities of Hiroshima and Nagasaki. The cities were almost completely wiped out, and more than 100,000 people were killed. On September 2, 1945, Japan surrendered. With Germany's surrender a few months earlier, World War II was finally over.

"We have used [the atomic bomb] against those who attacked us without warning at Pearl Harbor.... We have used it in order to shorten the agony of war, in order to save the lives of thousands and thousands of young Americans."

Harry S. Truman, who became president in April 1945 upon the death of President Roosevelt, describing the atomic bombs

◀ *The Japanese officially surrendered on the battleship USS* Missouri, *which is now a museum ship in Pearl Harbor.*

allies: countries who help each other in times of war

War at Home

In the United States, the war had created hardship for Americans of Japanese heritage. After Pearl Harbor was attacked, many Americans did not trust Japanese people living in the United States. Americans feared the Japanese were spying on them or would try to hurt them. So President Roosevelt had Japanese-Americans sent to guarded **internment** camps.

▼ *Japanese-Americans were kept in internment camps until after World War II ended.*

Ripped from Their Homes

More than 110,000 Japanese, including children, were shipped to these War Relocation Camps. Called "enemy aliens," some were immigrants from Japan, but nearly two thirds of the prisoners were American citizens. Some families took a few belongings with them, but many had only the clothes on their backs. For the rest of the war, they were forced to live in dirty, crowded buildings with little food to eat.

"If we were put there for our protection, why were the guns at the guard towers pointed inward, instead of outward?"

A Japanese prisoner in an internment camp; President Roosevelt told the Japanese he wanted to protect them from angry Americans

internment: being held against one's will, especially in wartime

Remember Pearl Harbor

Looking Back

More than 70 years after the attack on Pearl Harbor and after ten official investigations, people still have questions about that day of infamy. Why was America not ready for the attack? Were there clues that the Japanese were coming? Did the air raid on Pearl Harbor help or hurt Japan in the end?

▶ *Admiral Richmond Turner (left) was in charge of the War Plans Division at the time of the attack on Pearl Harbor.*

Early Warnings

Some people suspected that Japan might be planning to attack the United States. In February 1941, U.S. Admiral Richmond Turner warned that a "surprise attack upon the Fleet or Naval Base at Pearl Harbor" by Japan was "easily possible." Turner asked for Pearl Harbor to be put on high alert—but it was not.

▶ *Even though Admiral Yamamoto had advised against the attack on the United States, he became the face of the enemy to Americans.*

"We won a great tactical victory at Pearl Harbor and thereby lost the war."

Japanese Admiral Hara Tadaichi, voicing the common belief that the attack on Pearl Harbor put a huge target on Japan—which the Americans hit with atomic bombs

tactical: showing careful planning to achieve a goal

Missed Message

There were also warning signs much closer to the day of the attack. In early December, the United States cracked some coded messages from Japan. The Americans learned that Japan was planning a major Pacific strike. They did not know where or when the attack would take place, however. Most people believed that Japan would target the Philippines or Malaya—not Hawaii.

▶ *A deadly error was made when the Japanese planes approaching Pearl Harbor were mistaken for American planes.*

On Their Radar

About an hour before the attack, the American **radar** station in Oahu spotted a large group of planes heading to Hawaii from the north. A radar operator alerted the officer in charge right away. The equipment and the officer were both new to the job, and although he reported it, he was told the planes were American B-17 bombers. It was a grave mistake.

Some people believe that Roosevelt and the British prime minister Winston Churchill knew about Japan's plans to attack Pearl Harbor. They may not have alerted the U.S. Navy because they wanted the United States to join World War II. However, this idea has never been proven.

radar: a device used to track planes and other moving objects

Battle Cries

"Remember Pearl Harbor!" became a battle cry that pushed American troops to carry on during World War II. Today, people visit Pearl Harbor to remember the **victims** who died there. More than a million tourists visit the USS *Arizona* Memorial in Hawaii each year.

◀ *Americans wore buttons like this during the war, to remember what their country was fighting for.*

In 1988, an Act of Congress was passed that said the United States had been wrong to imprison Japanese-Americans after the attack. It gave compensation to the families. In 1991, President George W. Bush issued a formal apology for the government's actions at that time.

Tears of the *Arizona*

The USS *Arizona* was filled with oil when it sank in Pearl Harbor so long ago. Today, drops of the oil still bubble up from the wreck every day, closely monitored by the National Park Service. People call the drops the "tears of the *Arizona*." In 1999, the USS *Missouri*—the battleship on which the Japanese officially surrendered—was moored next to the *Arizona* at Pearl Harbor.

▼ *Many visitors pay their respects at the USS* Arizona *Memorial in Pearl Harbor, where the sunken ship can be seen in the water.*

victims: people who are hurt or killed in an attack

Learning More

Books

Day of Infamy: Attack on Pearl Harbor (Graphic History)
by Steve White
(Osprey Publishing, 2007)

I Survived the Bombing of Pearl Harbor, 1941
by Lauren Tarshis
(Scholastic Paperbacks, 2011)

The Attack on Pearl Harbor: An Interactive History Adventure
by Allison Lassieur
(You Choose Books, 2008)

Voices of Pearl Harbor
by Sherry Garland
(Pelican Publishing, 2013)

What Was Pearl Harbor?
by Patricia Brennan Demuth
(Grosset & Dunlap, 2013)

Movies

Pearl Harbor
A popular 2001 fiction film about the attack.

Websites

http://education.nationalgeographic.com/education/news/date-which-will-live-infamy/?ar_a=1
National Geographic: Date Which Will Live in Infamy

http://education.nationalgeographic.com/education/multimedia/interactive/pearl-harbor/?ar_a=1
National Geographic: Interactive Pearl Harbor Attack Map

www.nps.gov/valr/index.htm
National Park Service: World War II Valor in the Pacific

www.pbs.org/perilousfight/battlefield/pearl_harbor/letters/
PBS: The Perilous Fight

http://teacher.scholastic.com/pearl/index.htm#
Scholastic: We Witnessed the Attack on Pearl Harbor

Glossary

abandoned Left behind

air raid An attack by enemy planes

alerted Warned of danger

allies Countries who help each other in times of war

ambush To attack by surprise

ammunition Bullets and shells fired from weapons

beach To run a ship onto shore

bombarded Attacked repeatedly with bombs

civilians People who are not in the armed forces

colonies Places ruled by faraway leaders

economy The money and resources in a country

embargo A government order to stop trading with a country

empire A large area of land that is ruled by one leader

fleet A group of warships that sail and work together

infamy Being famous for something bad

internment Being held against one's will, especially in wartime

magazine A place where explosives are stored on a ship

radar A device used to track planes and other moving objects

tactical Showing careful planning to achieve a goal

victims People who are hurt or killed in an attack

victory The act of winning

Index

Entries in **bold** refer to pictures